The Spark Fi...

Book 7

Light and Wrong

Illustrated by Philip Reeve

DUCKPOOL:
125,000,000,
000,000 KM

ff

faber and faber

First published in 1999
by Faber and Faber Limited
3 Queen Square, London WCIN 3AU

Printed in Italy

Origination: Miles Kelly Publishing
Page layout: Mackerel

A CIP record for this book
is available from the British Library

ISBN 0-571-19742-6

0571 - 197 - 426 - 9909

For my nephews Owen and David, with love. BA

Be a Safe Scientist

DON'T FORGET TO WASH YOUR HANDS AFTER HANDLING PLANTS...

BE CAREFUL WHEN DOING ANY CUTTING OUT...

RRRRRAAAAWRR!

MAKE SURE AN ADULT IS AROUND IF YOU ARE LIGHTING CANDLES...

CAREFUL NOW...

Light and Wrong

FILE 1

NAME: Sam Spark
(that's me!)

DESCRIPTION: Brave, fearless and courageous. Single-handed I solved the Duckpool UFO mystery.

NOTES: We're the scientific Sparks
And you can call me Sammy.
I'm the best brain in our house
It's true! I really ammy!

FILE 2

NAME: Simon Spark
(my soppy brother)

DESCRIPTION: Useful for carrying stuff.
Looks like a mud pile –
and smells like one.
Helped me out a bit.

NOTES: Heroes need a right-hand man,
And mine is brother Simon
Brave and loyal and eager too
But difficult to rhyme on.

FILE 3

NAME: Mr Planck
(Duckpool
School Science teacher)

DESCRIPTION: New Science teacher.
Listens to us kids —
Very strange behaviour!
Has pet geranium
called Gerald!

NOTES: You never see a teacher dressed
As smart and bright as he is.
He's good at his experiments
But not as good as we is!

FILE 4

NAME: Bluto the Alien →

DESCRIPTION:
Very round
Very clever
Very annoying
And very stuck on Earth.

NOTES:
Marooned and left here on this earth
Our alien friend's a sphere
Except he has two dozen legs.
His boots must cost him dear!

Chapter 1

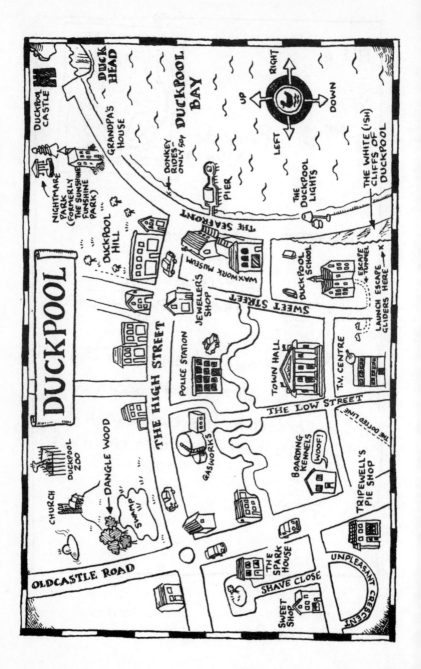

I was woken in the dead of night by the sound of a distant whirring. The sky was full of flickering lights. It looked like a meteor storm but we weren't due to see one. It was all very odd. A steady thump... thump... thump came from my bed. I carefully stretched out my hand and a huge wet tongue slobbered all over my arm. It was our dog, Boozle. He always crawls onto my bed when something scares him. Perhaps the noises and lights outside had worried him. "Boozle. Stop thumping your tail on the wall. You'll wake everyone up," I whispered. "I know you're worried but I have other things to worry about."

We were going to have a new science teacher at Duckpool School. It's not that I mind having a new teacher. It's just that it takes so long to train them. The first thing they do is shift everything around in the classroom. And you're supposed to know where it's been moved to. It's weeks before you can find anything. That's why I never tidy my bedroom. I can find things when it's a mess but once I tidy it then stuff disappears for ever. Why do adults have this thing about keeping bedrooms tidy? Perhaps I'll start a campaign. Leave Your Children's Rooms Alone or LYCRA – but that could be stretching things a bit.

Breakfast the next morning was the usual Sparks chaos. Gran was talking to the man on the radio.

WE ARE GETTING REPORTS FROM MANY LISTENERS THAT LAST NIGHT THEY HEARD STRANGE NOISES AND SAW UNUSUAL LIGHTS OVER DUCKPOOL. IF ANYONE SAW OR HEARD ANYTHING WILL THEY PLEASE PHONE THE RADIO STATION IMMEDIATELY...

"It's that nice man with all the good news," she said. "I don't like it when Sue Crawley is on, it's always bad news."

"Gran, it's not the news reader that decides whether the news is good or bad," my sister Sally tried to explain.

"Weather." Gran interrupted. "That's another thing. It's always bad when Jim Flood is on. With a name like that it's asking for trouble."

"Gran, it's got nothing to do with their name," Sally tried again.

"I like that new weather girl on TV," Gran continued. "We've had some lovely weather since she started."

"I think you mean weather woman," suggested Susie, my other sister.

"I tell you," Gran said, "if I lived in an area with a weather man called Bill Hurricane then I'd move. It wouldn't be safe."

"I saw some strange lights last night," I said.

"You were probably dreaming," Susie suggested.

"I don't think so. I got out of bed and looked out of the window. Simon, did you see anything?" I asked.

"No, nothing," he answered.

Now, I would have thought he would have heard the noises as well. After all, we do sleep in the same bedroom. Come to think of it, I don't remember seeing him in his bed when I got up to look at the lights. Perhaps he was sleepwalking again. Or more likely having a little snack from the fridge.

"Who's been at this trifle?" Gran's head emerged from the fridge.

"Not me," said Sally quickly.

"Or me," said Susie.

"Well it hasn't developed legs and walked, has it?" she snarled.

It wasn't good news when Gran was difficult this early in the morning.

"Gran, what do you think those strange lights were last night?" I asked.

"Could be all sorts of things," she answered. I'd managed to distract her from the missing trifle. "You can't always believe your eyes, you know."

"But I've got really good eyesight," said Susie.

"Ah, but your eyes can be fooled." Gran delved into her handbag and brought out a mangled old magazine.

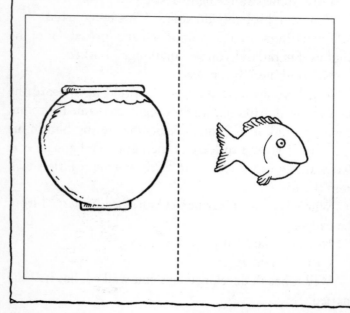

For the forward-thinking woman   *July 1955*

Don't always believe everything you are told or everything that you see. Remember you need to make up your own mind. Look at the picture below.

Cut out a piece of card 85mm by 70mm. Place your piece of card upright on the dotted line.

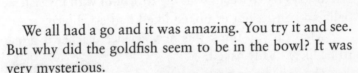

Now put your nose on the top of the card and look at the pictures.

What did you think you would see?

What did you see?

Now read the rest of the article to find out why you saw the goldfish in the bowl.

We all had a go and it was amazing. You try it and see. But why did the goldfish seem to be in the bowl? It was very mysterious.

"You see, you can't always believe your eyes," said Gran. She disappeared back into the fridge.

"Who's had the pork pie? I was having that for my lunch," she shouted. "I'm going to throttle the person that took my pie."

"RUN," I shouted.

We grabbed our bags and raced for the door.

"I'll throttle the lot of you when I catch you."

Chapter 2

We dived out of the front door and hurtled down the path. Gran was panting behind us and Boozle was dancing down the middle of the road. When we reached the corner we looked round and saw Gran talking to Mrs Mangle at Number 3. We were safe... until we got home again.

I always try to avoid walking to school with my sisters, Sally and Susie, but it looked like I had no choice.

"What do you think this new science teacher is going to be like?" Sally asked.

"Those lights in the sky last night were a bit odd," said Susie.

"I hope he likes science as much as we do," Sally continued.

"I reckon there's got to be an explanation for these things," Susie carried on.

Have you ever noticed how girls talk but don't listen? I tell you, I'm glad I'm a boy.

As we passed the newsagents, the poster outside looked interesting.

All my family is very interested in science. But I'd never heard of a Ufologist. Perhaps the new science teacher would know.

At school we all trooped into assembly and Mr Ramsbottom introduced the new teacher. I should explain that Mr Ramsbottom is very old, at least 54 years old, and is a doddering old twit. But he's our doddering old twit and we are quite fond of him. He taught our parents, or in Dad's case, tried to teach him.

"Well, children, isn't it a lovely day for discovering new things. We have a new teacher starting today who is going to help you in your quest for knowledge. Mr Planck will be taking over Miss Trout's teaching because she has very kindly agreed to help me to run the school. It's all very exciting. But then every day of one's life is full of excitement. Miss Trout will be the Acting Deputy Headteacher."

Elvis nudged me in the ribs and said, "I hope she's better at acting than she is at teaching." Elvis is my best friend but he doesn't have the brains that I've got... or the looks... or the genius... or the charm.

"Now, I want you lovely children to look after Mr Planck and make him feel welcome. Off to your classes and have a lovely day learning lots of new things. I'll come and see you all later. Come along, Miss Trout, we have some planning to do."

Miss Trout giggled and followed him.

We were the first class to meet the new science teacher. Mr Planck was tall and thin and very, very young. I know that as she gets older, Gran keeps saying the doctors and police officers are getting younger, but when your teachers get younger it's a bit worrying.

"Good morning, class. I am very much looking forward to teaching you this term," said Mr Planck.

"Hey, Sam, that's clever," Elvis nudged me again.

"It's what my Gran was on about this morning," I said. "You can't believe everything you see."

"That's exactly right," said Mr Planck. "Now, I want you all to make one of these. They are called thaumatropes."

Mr Planck handed out the worksheets with the instructions.

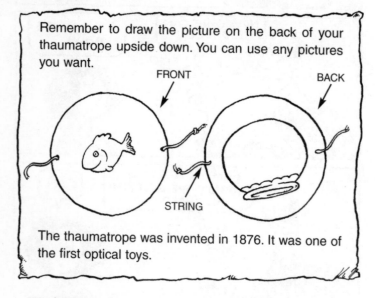

Remember to draw the picture on the back of your thaumatrope upside down. You can use any pictures you want.

FRONT

BACK

STRING

The thaumatrope was invented in 1876. It was one of the first optical toys.

We had a great time making the thaumatropes. Elvis made one that put a rabbit in a goldfish bowl!

Just before the end of the lesson Mr Planck uttered those dreaded words, "Your homework tonight..."

We all groaned.

"...is to show your thaumatropes to your family."

"Hey, Sam, this teacher might be OK."

Elvis' elbow jabbed at me again but I managed to avoid it for once. I decided that I might have to stop sitting next to Elvis. Apart from anything else I was getting sore ribs.

When I was walking home from school I started to think about our new science teacher. It was all very confusing. In school it's normally the teacher that does all the talking. It's my job to keep quiet and look intelligent. Of course, that's easy for me. Elvis, on the other hand, has a few problems with the looking intelligent bit. But Mr Planck appeared to listen to what we said. He even listened to Elvis! It just wasn't normal.

I told Gran about the new science teacher but she hadn't heard anything about him. This was getting really odd. My Gran knows about everyone in Duckpool. And what she doesn't know, she can find out. She had been to her welding class that day but no-one there mentioned the new teacher at Duckpool School. It was all very weird. Where had Mr Planck come from? And why was he so different from the other teachers?

"Gran, what's a Ufologist?" I asked at tea.

"It's a person who tries to track down Unidentified Flying Objects," she answered.

"But why is there a UFO researcher coming to Duckpool?"

"Loads of people reckon they saw unusual lights in the sky last night. The local radio's been going on about it all day. So they've got a Ufologist to come and investigate."

"But I still don't see why everyone's getting excited."

"Because some people think that UFOs are spaceships from other planets."

Aliens! In Duckpool? Wow!!

Chapter 3

I decided to ask Mr Planck about UFOs. Perhaps he knew something about them.

Elvis started the science lesson in his usual way... He fell off his chair. It's his party piece. He does it for all new teachers, a sort of welcome to Duckpool School. But Mr Planck just smiled at him and said,

"All of you close your eyes."

We closed our eyes.

"Now can you all hear me?"

We nodded.

"Can you all see me?"

We shook our heads.

"Am I still here?"

We nodded.

"He might not be," Elvis' voice rang out. "He might have gone out of the room. He might have set up a loudspeaker from the next room and be in there. He might have been kidnapped. And it might be the kidnapper who's talking to us. And the kidnapper might be planning to kidnap us as well."

"And he might be standing behind the boy who's talking."

"Aaaaaaarrrrrrrgggggggghhhhhhhh!!!!!!!!" screamed Elvis.

"What was the point of that experiment?" asked Mr Planck.

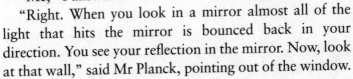

"So we could have a sleep," suggested Elvis.

"Good try, Elvis," replied Mr Planck.

"Sam, what do you see when you look in a mirror?"

"Me," I answered.

"Right. When you look in a mirror almost all of the light that hits the mirror is bounced back in your direction. You see your reflection in the mirror. Now, look at that wall," said Mr Planck, pointing out of the window.

We all stared at the wall.

"Can you see it?"

"Yes Sir," we all answered.

"Why can you see it?"

"Because I've got my eyes open," suggested Myrtle Brick.

"Good. But could you see it in the dark?"

"I could if I had a torch," said Myrtle.

Suddenly I could see what he was getting at. "We can see the wall because light is bounced off it into our eyes," I said.

"Exactly, well done. We only see light when it travels straight into our eyes," said Mr Planck. "Now I think I've told you enough. You will only learn about science by asking questions and doing lots of experiments. And remember there is always an explanation for everything. Now here's your homework."

We all groaned.

"Can you see around corners?"

"No," we all said.

"I want you to either make up or find an experiment that shows you why you can't see around corners."

"How are we supposed to do that?" asked Elvis.

"Do what a scientist does. Do some research. Use anything you can to find an answer. In this room there are books, videos, CD-ROMs, the Internet. Use whatever you can to find out. Be scientists. Use research to solve the problem."

Elvis and I searched through the videos but there wasn't anything useful there.

"Look, Elvis, you come round to my house tonight and we'll do a computer search."

That evening Elvis and I sat down in front of the computer. We typed the words LIGHT and CORNERS into the search and let the computer do the rest.

THREE HOLES AND A CANDLE

You need:
3 squares of card with a hole in the centre of each
a candle in a candle holder
a thin piece of dowel
some plasticine

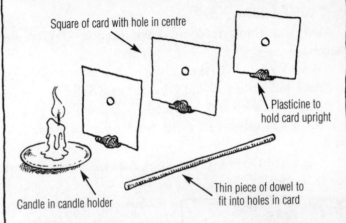

Square of card with hole in centre

Plasticine to hold card upright

Thin piece of dowel to fit into holes in card

Candle in candle holder

Make sure that you have lined up the holes in the cards so that you can see the candlelight. Push a piece of dowel through the holes. You will find that the dowel points straight at the candlelight.

This shows that light travels in straight lines.

We wandered downstairs to see if there was any food that needed taste-testing. It is my responsibility to check that all the food cooked in the house is suitable for the rest of the family. Well, that's my excuse and I'm sticking to it.

In the kitchen everyone was huddled around the radio.

"You know those lights you saw the other night," said Susie.

"Yeah," I answered.

"Do you think it could have been a UFO?" she suggested.

"What's a UFO?" asked Elvis.

"An Unidentified Flying Object," said Sally.

"And what's it for?" he asked.

"It's a spaceship for aliens from other planets," she said.

"Oh yeah! Do you really think that I am going to fall for that one?"

Susie explained that lots more people in Duckpool had been phoning the police and reporting that they had seen strange lights in the sky. Some of them reckon that they heard odd noises as well.

"That's probably their dogs snoring," I said.

"There could be something in it, you know," Sally joined in. "I was reading a book about UFOs and more and more people think they have seen them. It usually starts with lights in the sky and unusual noises. Then what often happens is that some people in the area are abducted by aliens."

"Well, no-one's abducting me," said Gran. "It's my bingo night and I'm not missing it for any aliens."

"Why would they want you, Gran?" I asked.

"There's a wise head on these shoulders, young lad. Just you remember that. Just because I'm old it doesn't mean that I'm useless."

I was on dangerous ground and I was hungry so I kept quiet. I noticed that my brother Simon was unusually quiet. He was sitting at the kitchen table and smiling at his football.

"Fancy a kick around, Simon?" I asked.

"No thanks," he replied and wandered out of the kitchen.

Now it's not like my brother to miss a chance of getting covered in mud. Perhaps he was ill. If he was, then I didn't want to catch it.

THE POLICE HAVE JUST ANNOUNCED THAT THEY WILL BE GETTING IN TOUCH WITH THE BRITISH UNIDENTIFIED FLYING OBJECT ORGANISED NETWORK. THEY ARE TAKING THE UFO SIGHTINGS VERY SERIOUSLY. IF ANYONE SEES ANY MORE STRANGE LIGHTS IN THE SKY, ESPECIALLY ABOVE DANGLE WOOD, THEN THE POLICE WOULD LIKE TO HEAR ABOUT THEM.

"They can't be serious," I said. "There's no such thing as UFOs. There's got to be a logical explanation."

"There's lots of things in this world that can't be explained," said Gran. "No-one believed your Grandad when he found the Duckpool Monster."

"The what?" asked Elvis.

"It was like the Loch Ness Monster but lived in the duckpool by the village green."

"Cor! That must have been exciting," Elvis was hooked.

"Don't listen to her, Elvis," I said. "She's crackers."

"That's right," she interrupted, "the Duckpool Monster was quackers."

We groaned.

Chapter 4

"Do you think I should tell the police about the lights I saw?" I asked.

"No!" shouted Simon from the hallway.

There was definitely something wrong with him. He was behaving very oddly. Yeah, I know he's odd most of the time. But this was different.

"Why do you say that?" I asked.

"There will be loads of people phoning the police. They will have enough information. One more bit won't make any difference," Simon explained.

"I'm not so sure," Sally interrupted. "It could be your piece of information that is vital to solving the mystery. I think you should tell the police. Let them decide if it's important or not."

"Gran, do you think the police will want to come round here?" asked Simon tentatively.

"I wouldn't think so. They'll be too busy to bother with us."

I went to phone the police and report what I had seen and heard. Simon was right. They didn't seem particularly interested. But the police officer said that I was right to report it.

The television news the next morning was full of UFO sightings in Duckpool. Overnight lots more people had spotted bright lights in the sky or had heard weird noises. Many had been woken from their sleep by the sounds and some of those interviewed on television looked terrified.

HERE I AM OUTSIDE THE RED LION PUBLIC HOUSE ON THE EDGE OF DANGLE WOOD IN DUCKPOOL WHERE A NUMBER OF THE LOCALS HAVE REPORTED SEEING UFOs

THE NUMBER OF SIGHTINGS SEEMS TO BE GROWING EVERY NIGHT AND THE MAYOR IS THINKING OF SETTING UP AN ADVICE LINE FOR LOCAL RESIDENTS WHO ARE WORRIED THAT THEY MIGHT BE ABDUCTED BY ALIENS. THERE IS FEAR IN THE AIR AND A STILLNESS HANGS OVER THE TOWN...

I AM JOINED NOW BY THE COUNTRY'S LEADING EXPERT ON UFO SIGHTINGS, PENNY HANDLES. MISS HANDLES, HOW SERIOUS ARE THESE SIGHTINGS?

WE ARE TAKING THEM VERY SERIOUSLY. IT SEEMS HIGHLY UNLIKELY TO US THAT THESE SIGHTINGS ARE A HOAX.

WE HAVE SET UP A SPECIAL ROOM IN THE RED LION AND ARE ASKING ALL PEOPLE WHO HAVE SIGHTED THE UFOS TO COME AND TALK TO US.

IS THERE ANY DANGER PEOPLE MIGHT BE ABDUCTED?

IT'S NOT VERY LIKELY BUT IT IS POSSIBLE.

"What a load of old rubbish," Gran declared. "Those sorts of comments will scare people. It shouldn't be allowed. I'm very tempted to phone the television company up and give them a piece of my mind."

"But what if there really are UFOs over Duckpool, Gran?" I asked.

"Don't be ridiculous," she said. "UFOs only started to be sighted about a hundred years ago. Are you telling me that aliens only learnt to build aircraft at the same time that we did?"

"What do you mean?" I asked.

"Look at this," Sally explained. "I've been doing a little research on the subject. I showed it to Gran earlier."

CACTUS GULCH GAZETTE

JANUARY 1887

ONLY 2 CENTS!

GULCH GOBSMACKED BY GHOSTLY GASBAGS!

One of the mystery airships that have baffled America was seen in the skies over Cactus Gulch this week. Rancher Jefferson P. Floss said, "Yup, it was enormous. It hovered over my barn and startled my cows with a powerful electric searchlight. I was so scared that my socks turned white overnight."

Thousands of people have been reported as seeing the flying airships that are taking over our night skies. Are they from another country? Are they from another world? Are they from another universe? These are the questions that our scientists are trying to answer.

SPECIAL REPORT

TERRIFYING MONSTER SIGHTED IN DUCKPOOL, ENGLAND!

FULL STORY ON PAGES 12, 14 & 27!

29

"Cor! That's amazing. So they had UFOs in 1887," I said. "But why hasn't someone found out what they are?"

"Listen, idiot brother. Keep your mouth shut and give your brain cell a chance."

Sally explained that no-one saw any airships in the skies over America until years later. In 1887 the only powered airships were in Europe but the Americans had heard about them. So when they saw anything in the sky that they couldn't understand, they thought it was an airship. These were not thought to be UFOs. That craze didn't start until after World War II.

"So all these sightings can all be explained," I said. "I suppose I must have seen a meteor storm. Which is what I thought it was in the first place."

At school everyone was talking about the UFO sightings. But I kept quiet. I didn't want anyone to know that I'd seen the bright lights. After all, I knew the truth.

Mr Planck didn't seem interested in the sightings either. He was more interested in the geraniums he had brought to school with him. When we walked into the classroom he was talking to them.

"Now, you'll be very happy here. I know I've moved you around a lot of times recently but this time we are here to stay for a while. Have a look at the view.

You'll get lots of sun on this windowsill and I'll still talk to you every day. Perhaps some of the children will get to care for you as I do. Then you'll have other people to talk to as well."

I looked at Elvis and shivered. This new teacher was behaving in a very odd way. But then all teachers are odd, so why should I worry?

"What are we doing today?" asked Elvis.

"You are going to make a pinhole camera."

"That's great, cos my camera got busted when I sat on it," said Elvis excitedly.

"I don't think we'll be making a real camera, Elvis," I said.

"But first, what did you all find out for homework?" asked Mr Planck.

We showed him our various experiments and all the information we found out. And in the end we all came up with the same answer. Light travels in straight lines.

Mr Planck drew a pinhole camera on the board for us so that we knew how to make one. But then we had to decide what we could use it for. Elvis decided he was going to take photos of himself and give them to all his friends. I kept trying to tell him that it wasn't a real camera. But sometimes Elvis is hard work.

You should make one of these. It's incredible. The picture at the end of the camera is upside down. Go on, try it and see. But the really amazing thing is that the same thing happens in your eye. The thing you are

31

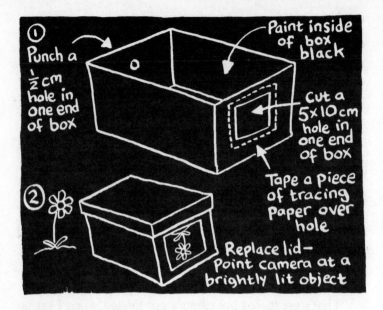

① Punch a ½ cm hole in one end of box

Paint inside of box black

Cut a 5×10 cm hole in one end of box

Tape a piece of tracing paper over hole

② Replace lid— Point camera at a brightly lit object

looking at ends up upside down at the back of your eye. It's your brain that unscrambles it. And then you see it the right way up.

"See, Elvis, just because you think you can see something, it doesn't mean that it's there," I said. "It's all in your head."

"Well, I can see my crisps in my bag and they'd better be there."

"But what if they aren't?"

"If my crisps aren't there, then it means someone has nicked them. And that means that someone is going to get battered."

Chapter 5

On my way out of school my brother Simon came hurtling up to me.

"Sam! Sam! I need to talk to you. It's very urgent." Simon grabbed me by the shoulder and dragged me behind the shed.

"I've got to talk to someone. I can't keep it a secret any longer."

"What are you on about, gnat brain?" I asked reasonably.

"Can you keep a secret?"

"What's it worth?"

"This is no time to mess around." Simon looked desperate. "There's something I've got to show you. It's in here."

Simon opened the door of the shed. Now, the last time he got me to go in that shed there was a bucket of water balanced on the door. When I walked in, I got soaked. I was not going to get caught by that again.

"After you," I said and stood back.

Simon led the way into the gloomy shed. Cobwebs brushed my cheek and dust settled on my clothes.

"So what is it?" I asked.

"It's there," he said, pointing to his new football.

"Is it possible you have been abducted by aliens and they wiped all your memory?" I asked. "It's your new football, you twit."

"This is no joking matter. Look carefully at the football."

I peered at the ball. And very slowly a leg started to appear. Then another. And another. And another... There must have been 50 of them.

I opened my mouth to scream as Simon clapped his hand over my mouth.

"It's... it's... it's... it's got legs," I gibbered. "It's Bluto from Pluto. My friend!"

"You know each other?" gasped Simon.

"How did you get here, Bluto?" I asked.

Bluto explained to me that the lights I saw were from his alien spaceship. When it landed, he got out of the ship with some of his mates for a roll around and then it took off before he had time to get on board. He rolled to our garden looking for me, but found my idiot brother Simon instead.

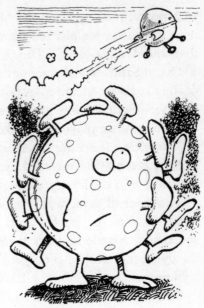

"But Bluto, you seem a lot smaller than you did on Pluto. Have you been on a diet?"

"No. I can make myself bigger and smaller but I can't alter my basic shape," Bluto explained.

"Wow!"

"Bluto was supposed to get back on his spaceship a couple of nights ago," interrupted Simon, "but all this UFO stuff means that there's hundreds of people out every night looking up at the skies. The spaceship can't risk landing and he's stuck here with us."

"We've got to help him," I declared. "We need to hide him until all this UFO scare is over."

"Oh, that's all rubbish," said Simon.

"How do you know the UFO stuff is rubbish?"

"Because Bluto says so."

"So all we do is go to the police and say, 'Look here, all this stuff about UFOs is rubbish, so will you please stop people looking up at the night sky?' When they ask how we know, we just tell them an alien told us. Yeah, that sounds reasonable... They'll lock us up, you lunatic!"

"Sam! Sam!" Elvis' voice cut through the air. The door of the shed opened and Elvis bounded in. "Come on, you two, we've got a footie game set up. You're on my side."

"Who are we playing?" I asked.

"Myrtle's got a team together," he said.

"I'm not playing them," I moaned. "The last time we played them I couldn't walk for a week."

The football game was a massacre. There were bodies lying all over the pitch – and some of them were the spectators. Myrtle and her team were winning 25–0. In the dying minutes we got a penalty and a chance to get a solitary goal.

"Sam, you take the penalty," shouted Elvis. "And use Simon's new football. It might bring us luck."

He threw me the football that had been sitting quietly on top of our sweaters.

LOOK! A UFO !!

Simon grabbed the football and we raced home together. That had been a close one.

The discussion at teatime was still about the UFOs. Simon and I tried to keep very quiet. Susie and Sally were convinced that it was a hoax.

"Look, I reckon it's something to do with light," said Sally. "Just because you think you see something then it doesn't mean that it's there. I need to know more about the way light works."

"Well, that's easy," I said. "Light goes in straight lines. And it can be bounced off a shiny surface – like a mirror."

"So why does this pencil look like it bends when I put it in the goldfish bowl?" Sally asked.

She had a point – and so did the pencil – it did look like it was bent. This was all very odd.

"Does this help?" Simon asked as he handed over his *Modern Magician's Mate*.

Try this on your friends. We guarantee they will be amazed...
Or your money back.

FIND THE MONEY

Put a coin in a bowl. Get your friend to look over the rim. Get her to slowly bend forward until the coin disappears.

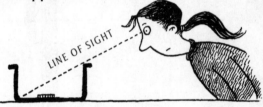

LINE OF SIGHT

Now pour some water into the bowl. Your friend will be amazed when she sees the coin reappear.

What happened was that the light reflected from the coin was bent towards your friend as it passed from the water into the air. This is why your friend could see a coin that she thought had disappeared.

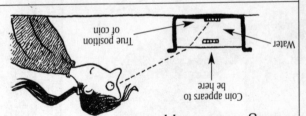

Coin appears to be here

Water

True position of coin

But remember, 'Shhhhh!' don't tell anyone your Magician's secrets.

This was all very interesting but it still didn't solve the problem. And we still had to try and get Bluto back on his ship. It was all getting too much for me when there was a loud knock at the door. When I answered it there were two men dressed in black.

"We'd like to speak to Sam Spark."

"G-U-L-P!!!"

Chapter 6

"Gran!" I shouted and ran into the kitchen.

"What's the matter?" she asked.

The men peered round the kitchen door.

"Excuse me, madam. We'd like a word with young Sam," one of them said. "We are investigating the UFO sightings."

"I'm sorry, but he's too busy at the moment," she answered. "You'll have to come back another time."

"But we won't take long," said the man in black.

"Maybe he will have time tomorrow. Come back then. Sally, show these men to the door."

When I heard the front door close I said to Gran, "Why wouldn't you let me speak to them?"

"Well, for one thing they didn't have any identification cards. So how do we know who they are? And for another, Mrs Hazel was telling me about how some strange men visited their Alfie after he'd reported seeing a UFO. Now Alfie didn't tell her about it, he wrote about it in his diary. She photocopied it to show me."

Today was the worst day of my life - even worse than the day Duckpool United got relegated. It was my tea break and I'd just opened my sandwich box to choose some food when a huge shape cast its shadow over me. I looked up and saw the outline of a man dressed all in black. Standing behind him was a second man — dressed exactly the same.

They told me to follow them so I got to my feet and followed. I didn't want to go but they seemed to have some sort of control over me. I looked back at my workmates but they seemed ~~were~~ unaware of what was happening. Only I could see the Men in Black.

They took me to a shiny black helicopter and I climbed inside. We travelled for what seemed like only a

few minutes but when we landed
it was on a bed of snow and
ice. The Men in Black (MIB)
climbed out and I followed.
I was
frozen
and
shivering.
The MIB didn't seem to notice the
cold. I was terrified. Would they
leave me there to freeze to death?
What did they want? What
had I done? They asked me
about the UFO that I'd seen.
They wanted to know how the
doors had opened. And they
wanted to know whom I'd seen.
One of them took a coin from
his pocket and crushed it to
dust in his hand. He said,
"The same thing will happen to
your heart if you tell
anyone about us, or the
UFO."
A few minutes in the helicopter
found us back at my work. I
can never tell this story to
anyone so this is why I
am writing it in my diary.

Gran put down the photocopy and looked at me.

"I think you might have had a close shave there, young lad," she said.

I was feeling sick. It was time to go to bed... and hide. For once I was glad that Boozle was sleeping on my bed.

But we still hadn't solved the problem of the alien. What were we going to do with him when we went to school the next day? Just as I was dropping off to sleep, Simon said, "Bluto can change into anything, you know. So long as it's shaped like a football."

On the way to school the next day we explained to Bluto that he would have to stop looking like a football because it was too dangerous for him. Apart from that, we weren't allowed to take footballs into the classroom. Simon and I decided that I should look after him for the day. When I got in the science classroom I looked around

for something that Bluto could change into. The globe, that would do. I took out the old globe and hid it in a cupboard and gently slotted Bluto into place. He opened his eyes and had a look round.

"This is great," he said. "I was getting a bit tired of hiding in Simon's bag. Apart from anything else the smell in there is disgusting."

"Now keep your eyes shut. Keep your legs in. And don't say anything," I told him. "I'll come and fetch you at the end of the day."

When the lesson started I was convinced that Mr Planck had finally snapped.

I could see why he was a science teacher and not a music teacher!

"Did you know that there's gold at the end of a rainbow?" he asked.

Well, we'd all heard that but didn't believe it.

"I've decided that if you all make me a rainbow then we can find the end of them... and find all the gold," he said. "We'll all be rich beyond our wildest dreams."

Now how on earth – or anywhere else – were we supposed to make Potty Planck a rainbow? People started rummaging in drawers for a rainbow-making kit. Others looked through the video collection. Elvis tried searching the computer for rainbows but got distracted by the latest football results. Don't ask me – I don't know how he got that either.

"Pssssst!"

I looked round.

"Pssssst! I know how to make a rainbow." The globe was whispering to me. I leaned casually against the cupboard with my back to the globe.

"I'm listening," I whispered back while trying to look like I was concentrating on a poster on the opposite wall.

I listened very carefully and... made a rainbow. Mr Planck was so impressed he asked me to show the whole class.

"That's brilliant, Sam!" shouted Mr Planck from the back of the classroom. "I think we'll leave the hunt for the pot of gold for another lesson. I must be teaching the cleverest children in the whole world." On the word 'world' he reached out his hand and spun the globe. I heard a faint, "Aaarrrrrgggghhh!!!" from Bluto.

When Mr Planck wasn't looking I skulked over to Bluto. He was still looking a bit green after his spin.

"I'll tell you one thing," he moaned. Space travel is nowhere near as bad as being a globe. Ooooh!! I do feel sick!"

Chapter 7

It was getting very difficult to hide Bluto at school. It was all going well until Elvis asked a question.

"Mr Planck," said Elvis, "What do you think about all these UFO sightings?"

"Well, they're obviously a load of rubbish. There's no life on any other planet."

"Yes, there is," muttered Bluto.

Mr Planck was looking round the class to see who was talking.

"No aliens could possibly be as intelligent as us."

"Yes they can."

"After all, we've only recently managed to fly into space," he went on.

"That's because you're all stupid."

By now Mr Planck was glaring at us. He couldn't work out who was talking. And how was I supposed to tell him that it was an alien disguised as a globe? After all, what teacher in their right mind – if any of them are – would believe that?

"Who's that talking?" Mr Planck asked angrily.

"It's not us," insisted Elvis. "Perhaps it's an alien hidden in a cupboard. Perhaps that's why the UFOs are here. I'll bet they are leaving loads of aliens to spend their time in lessons irritating the teachers," Elvis suggested.

"I think you can manage that on your own," said Mr Planck through gritted teeth.

I was glad when the lesson was over and I could hide Bluto in the shed.

I was beginning to get sick of all the talk about the UFO sightings. The evening television news was full of it again. It seemed that everyone in Duckpool had seen a UFO and some people reckoned they had been chatting to the aliens. Their roving reporter appeared to have roved all over the town collecting bizarre stories.

IT WAS INCREDIBLE! I WAS WALKING THE DOG WHEN HE STARTED TO GROWL. I LOOKED UP AND THERE WAS A HUGE DARK SAUCER SHAPE IN THE SKY.

IN THE DEAD OF NIGHT I WAS WOKEN BY ODD NOISES IN THE WOODS. WHEN I LOOKED OUT OF MY WINDOW I SAW A GROUP OF STRANGE PEOPLE DARTING BEHIND THE TREES...

I'VE NEVER SEEN ANYTHING LIKE IT BEFORE AND NEVER WANT TO AGAIN. IT WAS TALLER THAN ME AND COVERED WITH SCALES. ITS HEAD WAS ENORMOUS AND IT LOOKED AT ME WITH GLARING BLACK EYES!

Even the new weather girl, Sondra, was doing her report from Duckpool. I thought it was all getting very silly. But then, I did know what a real alien looked like. What was really odd was that lots of people reported seeing a group of aliens in Dangle Wood. Now, most locals keep away from there. Too many dogs have got stuck in the swamp and the fire officers are sick of rescuing them. I knew that it wasn't aliens in the woods – because the only alien that had landed was asleep in our shed. So who could it possibly be that kept being seen in Dangle Wood? There was no way that I was going there at night but we needed someone to go. Who did I know that was daft enough to go to Dangle Wood at night?

"Simon," I called. "I've got a job for you."

Unfortunately Simon is not as stupid as he looks. Well, it would be difficult to be that stupid. But very unreasonably, I thought, he refused to go to Dangle Wood. I tried all my powers of persuasion. I asked him nicely. Then I asked him not so nicely. Then I sat on his head. Then I got Boozle to sit on his head. But nothing worked.

At school the next day I tried to convince Elvis that a night hike was a good idea. He thought it was brilliant as well until he found out where I wanted him to hike to. Sometimes you just can't rely on anyone. It was no good, I would have to go to Dangle Wood myself... and take Boozle... and Bluto...  and a torch... and maybe Simon and Elvis. After all, there's no point in taking any risks when there's UFOs involved.

In science Mr Planck looked exhausted. His face was as green and shiny as his waistcoat. He must have been up all night marking our homework.

"What would happen if it was dark all the time?" he asked.

"I'd trip over things," said Elvis.

"We wouldn't be able to play football."

"My hamster would be out all the time because he'd think it was night time."

"Bats would be flying around all the time."

"Those are all good answers. But what about plants?" Mr Planck asked.

A sea of blank faces stared back at him.

"Elvis, what are you having for tea tonight?" I was sure Mr Planck had finally flipped.

"Hamburger and chips," answered Elvis.

"What do you think my Gerald is having for his tea tonight?"

"He can have some of my chips if you want," suggested Elvis.

"Gerald is my geranium, Elvis," said Mr Planck. "He can't eat chips."

"I suppose he can't eat hamburger either," whispered Elvis.

"Gerald is very, very clever. He can make his own food," explained Mr Planck.

Elvis nudged me, "Do you think he could make me some? I'm starving."

"But even though Gerald is very, very clever he is not as clever as Jemima. She can make her own food and she can obey my instructions."

Mr Planck produced a shoebox from underneath his desk with a flourish like a magician.

"Would you like to see how clever Jemima is?"

"Yes, please," we all shouted. This should be good. A trained geranium.

Elvis and I looked at each other and groaned.

"Did you really think I had a trained geranium?" laughed Mr Planck. "You are daft sometimes."

It's a bad day when a teacher gets the better of you. But I don't forget things like that. One day I'd get my own back on Mr Planck.

It's really easy to make a plant maze. Try it and see. Make sure you keep the inside of the shoebox really dark so that the plant grows towards the hole in the lid. And you don't need to dress up as a ringmaster to make one!

But I didn't have time to make one – I had to plan the night trip to Dangle Wood. It would be dangerous and it would be frightening. But somebody had to do it. And that somebody was... me.

Chapter 8

In my bedroom, I collected together all the essentials for my trip into the dark and dingy Dangle Wood.

Warm clothes

Pencil →

← Notebook

← chocolates

Torch

Dog biscuits
(Those were for
Boozle not me)

I would wait until everyone was asleep and then sneak out of the house. I had decided not to take Simon as he's more trouble than he's worth, but Bluto was ready for his trip. He wanted to use the time to try and contact his spaceship. And he needed to find a place for it to land. But first I needed to find Bluto. I'd left him in the cupboard, but he must have got bored and gone for a roll around. I checked the bedrooms, and the sitting room and the kitchen, and the garage, and... Well, I checked everywhere. I was beginning to think that he'd disappeared from the planet.

"Tea time," shouted Gran from the kitchen. "I've got a special treat for you all."

"I hope she hasn't been looking in that new cookbook of hers again," said Sally as we walked down the stairs. "That bean and marmalade casserole she made was disgusting."

My Gran is a brilliant cook provided she sticks to the recipe. But sometimes she doesn't have the right ingredients so she sticks in something the same colour. Sometimes it works and sometimes it doesn't. Replacing carrots with marmalade did not work.

On the kitchen table was a Christmas pudding, big enough to feed two armies.

"Gran, why are we having Christmas pudding in February?" I asked.

"Do you have to live in Brussels to eat Brussels sprouts? Or do you have to live in Dover to eat Dover sole? Or do you have to live in Eccles to eat Eccles cakes? Or do..."

"Yes, Gran," we shouted together, "We get the point."

I drooled at the Christmas pudding and... it winked back. It was Bluto. Gran had cooked him in the oven!

"Simon," I whispered. "That's Bluto. We've got to save him."

Simon leaned over to the Christmas pudding and peered at it. It peered back... and winked.

"Let's all make a wish," said Gran as she raised the knife high in the air. She was going to murder Bluto – and then we'd have to eat him. Yeuch!!!!

"Simon, do something!" I ordered.

Simon immediately fell backwards off his chair and crashed onto the kitchen floor. His face was grey and his body still and cold.

"Call an ambulance," screamed Gran.

Sally rushed to the phone and I rushed to the Christmas pudding. I grabbed it, opened the back door, and threw it out. Boozle loped after it.

"Where am I?" asked Simon. "What day is it? Am I lying on the ceiling or the floor?'

"Belt up, Simon. You can get up now," I said.

"Who are you, little boy?" asked Simon, his glazed eyes staring at me.

"Stop messing about and get up," I ordered.

He lay back with a stupid smile on his face. I mean a more stupid smile than usual.

"Sam, stop being so horrible," said Gran. "The poor lad has had a nasty bang on the head."

"Bang on the head," repeated Simon.

"I expect he's got concussion," she added.

"Concussion," he echoed.

I had to admit that Simon did look a bit rough. The ambulance crew must have thought so as well because they took him off to hospital – and Gran went too.

It was strangely lonely in my bedroom that night. Usually I want Simon to sleep somewhere else, but I seemed to be missing him. The hospital was keeping him overnight just to keep an eye on him. They seemed to think he was saying odd things. Nothing new there, I thought. But they were more worried that he kept seeing big green slimy lizards. I thought he'd probably been looking in the mirror.

I checked the supplies for my excursion and decided to take a magnifying glass. Then I remembered Simon had broken it when he was trying to look inside Boozle's ear. I was sure we must have a book that would help.

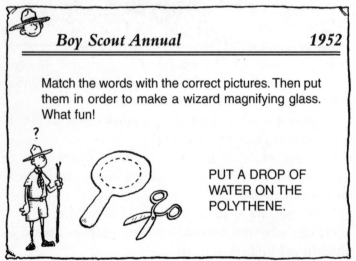

Boy Scout Annual 1952

Match the words with the correct pictures. Then put them in order to make a wizard magnifying glass. What fun!

PUT A DROP OF WATER ON THE POLYTHENE.

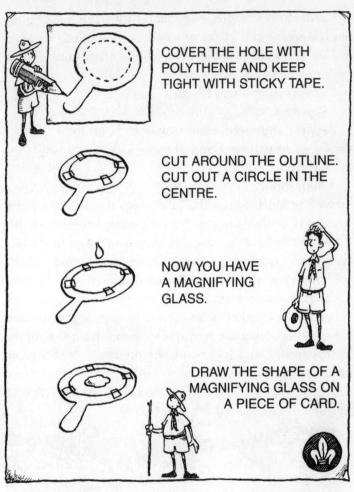

COVER THE HOLE WITH
POLYTHENE AND KEEP
TIGHT WITH STICKY TAPE.

CUT AROUND THE OUTLINE.
CUT OUT A CIRCLE IN THE
CENTRE.

NOW YOU HAVE
A MAGNIFYING
GLASS.

DRAW THE SHAPE OF A
MAGNIFYING GLASS ON
A PIECE OF CARD.

When everyone was asleep I woke Boozle and Bluto
and we sneaked off to Dangle Wood. I expected the roads
to be empty but we had to keep hiding behind trees
and walls to avoid all the people who were out looking
for the UFO. As we neared the wood it got quieter and
quieter... and darker and darker. All I could hear was
the sound of Boozle panting and my heart thudding in
my ears.

Suddenly Boozle froze and stood still. The hairs on his back were rigid and he growled quietly. Bluto stopped rolling and stretched out his telescopic legs until he was the same height as me.

"What can you see, Boozle?" I asked.

"Grrrrrrrr."

Between the tree trunks was a faint light. In the distance I heard the sound of humming.

"Grrrrrrr."

"Shhh, Boozle."

We tiptoed between the fallen logs towards the light. The fuzzy outlines in the distance started to take shape. I couldn't believe my eyes. A group of huge lizard-like creatures were dancing, their sequinned shells shimmering in the firelight. I turned and gazed in wonder at the strange creatures bobbing and weaving among each other like a blanket of maggots. Boozle began to bark furiously, ignoring my attempts to silence him. One of the lizards turned and looked in our direction. It started to lumber steadily towards us. I pulled Boozle and Bluto towards me and dragged them behind a huge log. We held our breath and waited for it to find us.

63

Chapter 9

We could hear the lizard shuffling through the undergrowth towards our hiding place. Any second we would be found. Would the lizard take us back to its camp? I'd read terrible stories about people being abducted by aliens. I didn't want the next person to be me. Would we ever get home again? I looked into Boozle's terrified eyes. As I turned my head to look at Bluto I noticed that he was smiling! How could he? We were about to be captured and dragged away, never to see our families again. Before I could stop him Bluto leapt from behind our log and bellowed at the lizard. The lizard screamed a spine-tingling scream and dived back through the trees.

"What did you do that for?" I asked.

Bluto was lying in the undergrowth howling with laughter.

"You idiot," I said. "He'll be back any minute with the rest of the lizards."

I grabbed Boozle's collar and we hurtled out of the wood. Bluto rolled behind us but I could hear him chuckling to himself. The sooner Bluto was back on his spaceship the better.

Back at home I clambered into bed with Boozle and hid, and Bluto rolled into his cupboard. I was never ever going to Dangle Wood again.

The next morning Simon arrived home from hospital looked a bit confused.

"I'm worried," he confided to me in our bedroom. "The doctors think that I may have something wrong with my brain."

"Are they sure you've got a brain?" I asked helpfully.

"This is serious. They want to do a brain scan on me."

"Why look at an empty space?"

"When I was in hospital I kept seeing a huge lizard in the distance," he persisted. "But no-one believed me. Now they think there's something wrong with my eyes or my brain. But I did see something. I'm sure of it."

"What did it look like?" I asked.

Somewhere recently I had seen something else that reminded me of a lizard. Should I tell someone about what I'd seen in Dangle Wood? But what was it?

At breakfast Gran fussed over Simon. He was still feeling a bit sick after his bang on the head, so Boozle and

I shared his breakfast. Boozle really loves bacon and eggs. I could still hear Bluto giggling softly in his cupboard. I wasn't going to waste my energy speaking to him. He had nearly got me killed so from now on he could look after himself.

Gran snapped on the radio to see if there had been any UFO developments. I kept very quiet.

MORE REPORTS ARE COMING IN THIS MORNING OF UFO SIGHTINGS OVERNIGHT. WE ARE ALSO GETTING INFORMATION ABOUT STRANGE GOINGS ON AT DANGLE WOOD. IT SEEMS LIKELY THAT THE ALIENS MAY BE HIDING IN THE WOOD. FIRST REPORTS INDICATE THAT THE ALIENS MAY LOOK LIKE LIZARDS. POLICE ARE VERY CONCERNED ABOUT THE SAFETY OF PEOPLE IN DUCKPOOL. I HAVE A STATEMENT FROM THE POLICE THAT I WILL NOW READ TO YOU: WE ADVISE ALL PARENTS TO KEEP THEIR CHILDREN AT HOME TODAY. ALL SCHOOLS IN DUCKPOOL ARE CLOSED UNTIL FURTHER NOTICE. KEEP LISTENING TO YOUR LOCAL NEWS FOR MORE INFORMATION.

"Hurrah!!" we all shouted. "School's closed!" We danced round the kitchen shouting and singing. Simon grabbed his football and dived for the door.

"Where do you think you're going?" asked Gran.

"To play footie with the lads."

"No way. You are staying at home. You heard what the police said."

This was not good news. School was closed but we were all stuck in the house for the day.

"Hang on a minute," said Simon. "Did they say the aliens looked like lizards?"

"Yes."

"See? I said I saw a lizard at the hospital."

"But what would a lizard alien be doing at the hospital?" I asked.

By now Bluto was howling with laughter. I opened the cupboard door.

"Belt up, Bluto. Someone might hear you," I ordered.

"Lizard aliens. It's hysterical. We all know that aliens can change their shape so why would they want to look like lizards?"

"But we saw them last night," I insisted.

"What do you mean, you saw them last night?" asked Simon.

It didn't take long to explain our jaunt to Dangle Wood.

"There's only one thing to do," said Simon. "We will have to go to Dangle Wood tonight and see what's really going on there. Bluto doesn't think that the lizards are aliens and I think he should know."

"I'm not going back there," I insisted. "It was terrifying. I am never ever going there again."

"We'll leave once it's dark," ordered Simon. "But we need a little more than a wonky magnifying glass and a torch. We need some way of watching what's going on while we are hiding."

"It would be very useful if we could see through trees," I said sarcastically.

"I can see through trees," said Bluto.

"What?"

"In fact, I can see through anything."

"Can you see through clothes?" I stammered.

"That's easy," he said.

"That's disgusting."

"But most of the time I don't look. After all, who wants to spend their time looking at Simon's underpants – even if they have got teddy bears on them?"

Simon glared at Bluto, "The sooner you go back on your spaceship the better."

For once my brother and I agreed about something. But we still needed something that would allow us to spy on the lizards without being seen. When in doubt, use the computer. That's my motto. It didn't take long to find what we needed.

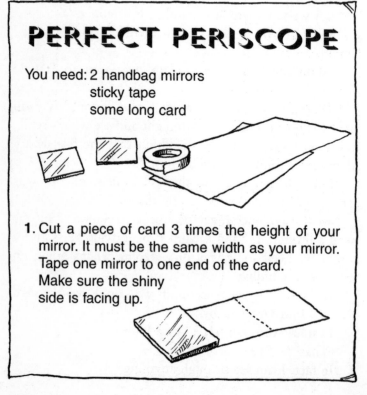

PERFECT PERISCOPE

You need: 2 handbag mirrors
           sticky tape
           some long card

1. Cut a piece of card 3 times the height of your mirror. It must be the same width as your mirror. Tape one mirror to one end of the card. Make sure the shiny side is facing up.

2. Fold the card into a triangular prism. Make sure one of the angles is a right angle. Tape the prism together.

Mirror

Right angle

3. Make another triangular prism using the second mirror.

4. Cut a large rectangle of card and fold into sections like this:

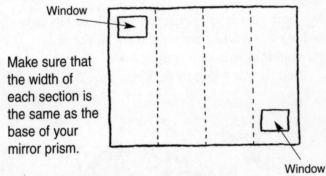

Window

Make sure that the width of each section is the same as the base of your mirror prism.

Window

5. Cut out the windows in the card.

6. Stick the card together to make a tube.

7. Put a mirror prism at each end of the tube with the mirror facing the window. Tape them in place.

Mirror → ← Window

Window → ← Mirror

We both made a periscope. At least it gave us something to do when we were stuck in the house. Then all we could do was wait until it was dark and everyone was asleep. It was going to be a very long day.

Chapter 10

It was a strange group that crept through the side streets and alleyways of Duckpool on the way to Dangle Wood. At least Bluto had stopped laughing. We heard police sirens in the distance and saw the flashing of blue lights on the ridge behind the pie factory. The police were still taking the UFO sightings very seriously. It didn't take long to find the lizards' camp.

"You see, I said I wasn't seeing things," insisted Simon as we settled down behind a fallen tree. Bluto transformed himself into a giant puffball fungus and sat on top of the log. The lizards were dancing again and making high-pitched sounds that upset Boozle. He whined and whimpered at the noise. Suddenly he started to sniff the air and wag his tail. Nearby was the sound of snapping twigs and rustling leaves. We followed the sound with our periscopes.

"Over there," Simon nudged me. "Bloodhounds."

He was right. The sniffer dogs slowly snuffled their way towards us. Boozle was getting more and more excited at the thought of having someone to play with. We might be able to hide from lizards but we had no chance of hiding from bloodhounds. The bloodhounds slobbered and drooled all over us. Seconds later the local television weather girl, Sondra, crawled out from behind a tree.

"Can you see anything?" she asked.

Simon sat staring at her like a goldfish looking for food.

"It's a bit late for weather forecasts, isn't it?" I said.

"I'm sick of doing the weather," she said. "I want to be a reporter but the TV station won't send me on any stories. So I decided to track down my own stories."

"Can I have your autograph?" asked Simon soppily.

"Belt up, you twit," I ordered.

I told Sondra all that we knew. I missed out the bit about Bluto. She borrowed my periscope and peered through the mist at the lizards.

"My Gran thinks you're wonderful." Simon gazed lovingly at Sondra with glazed eyes.

"I wish I had a camera with me," whispered Sondra. "Have you got one?"

"No, we haven't. I didn't think to bring one," I said. "Can't you get someone from the TV station down here with a camera?"

"I'll try. They should still be around after the last weather report I did," she answered and reached into her pocket for her mobile phone.

"Simon, stop rustling that paper," I snarled. "You're not having her autograph."

He poked his tongue out at me and smiled sweetly at Sondra. Seeing your little brother in love for the first time is a horrible sight.

"The camera crew's on its way," Sondra whispered. "They reckon that the police have tracked some of the aliens to this wood."

"Can I have my picture taken with you?" soppy Simon asked. "I'll stick it up over my bed."

Fortunately Sondra was ignoring Simon. I delved in the rucksack and found the chocolates and dog biscuits. Simon was so befuddled that he ate the dog biscuits. I didn't mind because that meant there were more chocolates for Sondra and me, but Boozle was a bit miffed. He lay down and grumbled under his breath.

The camera crew crawled like commandos through the leaf litter towards our position. It seemed a bit dramatic to me but that's television people for you. Sondra introduced us to Patsy and Sebastian.

"Right, Sondra. Let's do some opening shots from here," said Sebastian. "Then we'll move closer to the lizards. By the way, where are they?"

We pointed towards the campfire.

"Wow!!! What a great story," he gasped. "We'll be the first people to get real live aliens on film. I can see us winning prizes with this footage. Let's get it in the bag before anyone else turns up."

HERE WE ARE IN THE DEPTHS OF DANGEROUS DANGLE WOOD. WE'RE SURROUNDED BY THE NIGHT SOUNDS OF WILDLIFE IN PERIL. IN THE DISTANCE WE CAN SEE THE OUTLINES OF THE AWESOME ALIENS THAT THE PETRIFIED PEOPLE OF DUCKPOOL HAVE BEEN PLAGUED BY OVER RECENT DAYS. WITH ME I HAVE THE TWO HEROIC BOYS WHO FIRST DISCOVERED THE CREATURES' LAIR. IN YEARS TO COME THESE ALIENS SHOULD BE KNOWN AS THE **SPARK LIZARDS** IN RECOGNITION OF THE BRILLIANT WORK DONE BY THESE YOUNG LADS. WE ARE NOW GOING CLOSER TO THE LIZARDS' TERRITORY. WE NEED TO KEEP VERY, VERY QUIET AS WE CREEP FORWARD TO FILM THEM...

Sebastian swung his camera towards the lizards' lair and held it still while we held our breath.

"That's brilliant," he chortled. "Absolutely brilliant." He was howling with laughter.

"Shhh," I said. "The lizards will hear you."

"Look through the camera and you'll see what I mean." Sebastian handed me the camera. I looked and I saw. And then I knew the truth.

Chapter 11

"We've got to get this on film," I insisted. "Or no-one is going to believe us."

There was no time to waste. The lizards could get away before we got to them. We sneaked through the wood nearer and nearer to the lizards. Simon moaned and complained, "What if the lizards see us? What if they decide to eat us?"

"I won't let the lizards eat you," I whispered. "Trust me."

Sebastian grinned at me.

We were only a few metres away from the lizards when Sebastian spoke.

"Let's do an introduction from here. Then we can walk forward and interview the lizards," he suggested.

"Interview the lizards!" gulped Simon. "What makes you think they will understand you?"

"Trust me," said Sebastian.

"I wish people would stop saying that," whinged Simon. "It makes me nervous."

"We need this live on television," whispered Sebastian. "Give me a minute while I set up the link."

Sebastian picked up his mobile phone and made a series of calls. Soon we were ready and all of Duckpool would be watching on their televisions. This was Sondra's chance to be a television reporter.

> OVER THE PAST FEW DAYS DUCKPOOL HAS BEEN GRIPPED BY UFO FEVER. RUMOURS HAVE BEEN RIPPLING THROUGH THE TERRIFIED TOWN. WE ARE NOW ONLY A FEW METRES AWAY FROM THE LIZARDS' LAIR, THE CAUSE OF MANY OF THE ALIEN SIGHTINGS. I AM NOW GOING TO MOVE FORWARD AND INTERVIEW THEIR LEADER. THE TRUTH IS OVER THERE...

Sondra walked bravely towards the lizards. Their dancing was getting wilder and more frantic. As they swung each other round they whooped and howled into the night air. I just hoped that the rest of my family was watching this at home. Otherwise they'd never believe it.

77

The police appeared from nowhere. The lizards panicked and rushed around trying to get away. Unfortunately their lizard suits were not designed for swift movement and they crashed over tree stumps and each other's tails in their efforts to escape.

It didn't take the police long to round up the lizards and load them into a police van. I wish I could have been at the police station when they were interviewed.

As we walked back through the trees we saw Bluto gazing up at the stars.

"They'll be here tomorrow," he said wistfully. "I'll be going home."

But now we had to get home. It had been a long night and we were exhausted.

The next morning we were besieged by local reporters. They were hammering on the door very early asking for our version of the story. They wanted to know all about the lizards and how we knew they were fakes. Now, we could have told them what our friendly alien told us, but I don't think they would have believed us. The newspapers were full of the story and I got sick of seeing my picture on the television. During the day a series of programmes interviewed the experts and the lizards.

79

Suddenly I remembered where I'd seen that lizard skin before – Mr Planck's waistcoat. Things were beginning to slot into place but there were still some gaps.

"Gran, if the UFOs were a load of rubbish then how do you explain Alfie's diary?" I asked.

"It turns out that it was his homework for a creative writing course he's doing. He didn't want his Mum to know about his writing so he hid it in his diary.

"But why did I see a lizard at the hospital?" Simon asked.

"Because one of them was injured in Dangle Wood and was taken to hospital. He said he was going to a fancy dress party," Gran explained.

"So I'm not going mad," Simon sighed.

"I didn't say that!" Gran grinned.

So Mr Planck was right, there was an explanation for everything. But not always the explanation you expect.

The day was long and tiring but we couldn't go to bed

until Bluto had finally left us. After dark we again dragged ourselves to Dangle Wood where his spaceship was going to land.

"Isn't someone going to report seeing a UFO?" I asked.

"Even if someone does," he replied, "will the police take it seriously?"

He had a point. But I was going to miss Bluto. It may have been difficult hiding him and he was a pain in the neck at school but it was good to meet new and different people. And Bluto was definitely different.

To the second, the spaceship appeared in the sky and hovered over the wood. The door opened and a beam of light illuminated the ground. Bluto waved to us and stepped into the light. It sucked him into the ship and he was gone.

HA HA HA! HEE HEE HEE! HO HO!

As I walked home I wondered if I would ever see him again.

"Simon," I said sadly, "You know aliens can change their shape to look like anything?"

"Yeah."

"Then what's to stop that tree being an alien? Or that wall? Or that dog?"

"You're bonkers," he said.

"Perhaps I am, but I'm sure a postbox smiled at me last week."

83

Here is a list of the experiments in this book. Have you tried them all?

Science Notes

Science Notes

☀ Science Notes ☀

Science Notes

Science Notes